COMING ATTRACTION

Start Publishing PD LLC

Manufactured in the United States of America

Cover art: Shutterstock/Taisiya Kozorez

Cover design: Jennifer Do

10 9 8 7 6 5 4 3 2 1

ISBN 979-8-8809-0325-2

Coming Attraction

by Fritz Leiber

The coupe with the fishhooks welded to the fender shouldered up over the curb like the nose of a nightmare. The girl in its path stood frozen, her face probably stiff with fright under her mask. For once my reflexes weren't shy. I took a fast step toward her, grabbed her elbow, yanked her back. Her black skirt swirled out.

The big coupe shot by, its turbine humming. I glimpsed three faces. Something ripped. I felt the hot exhaust on my ankles as the big coupe swerved back into the street. A thick cloud like a black flower blossomed from its jouncing rear end, while from the fishhooks flew a black shimmering rag.

"Did they get you?" I asked the girl.

She had twisted around to look where the side of her skirt was torn away. She was wearing nylon tights.

"The hooks didn't touch me," she said shakily. "I guess I'm lucky."

I heard voices around us:

"Those kids! What'll they think up next?"

"They're a menace. They ought to be arrested."

Sirens screamed at a rising pitch as two motor-police, their rocket-assist jets full on, came whizzing toward us after the coupe. But the black flower had become a thick fog obscuring the whole street. The motor-police switched from rocket assists to rocket brakes and swerved to a stop near the smoke cloud.

"Are you English?" the girl asked me. "You have an English accent."

Her voice came shudderingly from behind the sleek black satin mask. I fancied her teeth must be chattering. Eyes that were perhaps blue searched my face from behind the black gauze covering the eyeholes of the mask. I told her she'd guessed right.

She stood close to me. "Will you come to my place tonight?" she asked rapidly. "I can't thank you now. And there's something you can help me about."

My arm, still lightly circling her waist, felt her body trembling. I was answering the plea in that as much as in her voice when I said, "Certainly." She gave me an address south of Inferno, an apartment number and a time. She asked me my name and I told her.

"Hey, you!"

I turned obediently to the policeman's shout. He shooed away the small clucking crowd of masked women and barefaced men. Coughing from the smoke that the black coupe had thrown out, he asked for my papers. I handed him the essential ones.

*

He looked at them and then at me. "British Barter? How long will you be in New York?"

Suppressing the urge to say, "For as short a time as possible," I told him I'd be here for a week or so.

"May need you as a witness," he explained. "Those kids can't use smoke on us. When they do that, we pull them in."

He seemed to think the smoke was the bad thing. "They tried to kill the lady," I pointed out.

He shook his head wisely. "They always pretend they're going to, but actually they just want to snag skirts. I've picked up rippers with as many as fifty skirt-snags tacked up in their rooms. Of course, sometimes they come a little too close."

I explained that if I hadn't yanked her out of the way, she'd have been hit by more than hooks. But he interrupted, "If she'd thought it was a real murder attempt, she'd have stayed here."

I looked around. It was true. She was gone.

"She was fearfully frightened," I told him.

"Who wouldn't be? Those kids would have scared old Stalin himself."

"I mean frightened of more than 'kids.' They didn't look like 'kids.'"

"What did they look like?"

I tried without much success to describe the three faces. A vague impression of viciousness and effeminacy doesn't mean much.

"Well, I could be wrong," he said finally. "Do you know the girl? Where she lives?"

"No," I half lied.

The other policeman hung up his radiophone and ambled toward us, kicking at the tendrils of dissipating smoke. The black cloud no longer hid the dingy facades with their five-year-old radiation flash-burns, and I could begin to make out the distant stump of the Empire State Building, thrusting up out of Inferno like a mangled finger.

"They haven't been picked up so far," the approaching policeman grumbled. "Left smoke for five blocks, from what Ryan says."

The first policeman shook his head. "That's bad," he observed solemnly.

I was feeling a bit uneasy and ashamed. An Englishman shouldn't lie, at least not on impulse.

"They sound like nasty customers," the first policeman continued in the same grim tone. "We'll need witnesses. Looks as if you may have to stay in New York longer than you expect."

I got the point. I said, "I forgot to show you all my papers," and handed him a few others, making sure there was a five dollar bill in among them.

*

When he handed them back a bit later, his voice was no longer ominous. My feelings of guilt vanished. To cement our relationship, I chatted with the two of them about their job.

"I suppose the masks give you some trouble," I observed. "Over in England we've been reading about your new crop of masked female bandits."

"Those things get exaggerated," the first policeman assured me. "It's the men masking as women that really mix us up. But, brother, when we nab them, we jump on them with both feet."

"And you get so you can spot women almost as well as if they had naked faces," the second policeman volunteered. "You know, hands and all that."

"Especially all that," the first agreed with a chuckle. "Say, is it true that some girls don't mask over in England?"

"A number of them have picked up the fashion," I told him. "Only a few, though—the ones who always adopt the latest style, however extreme."

"They're usually masked in the British newscasts."

"I imagine it's arranged that way out of deference to American taste," I confessed. "Actually, not very many do mask."

The second policeman considered that. "Girls going down the street bare from the neck up." It was not clear whether he viewed the prospect with relish or moral distaste. Likely both.

"A few members keep trying to persuade Parliament to enact a law forbidding all masking," I continued, talking perhaps a bit too much.

The second policeman shook his head. "What an idea. You know, masks are a pretty good thing, brother. Couple of years more and I'm going to make my wife wear hers around the house."

The first policeman shrugged. "If women were to stop wearing masks, in six weeks you wouldn't know the difference. You get used to anything, if enough people do or don't do it."

I agreed, rather regretfully, and left them. I turned north on Broadway (old Tenth Avenue, I believe) and walked rapidly until I was beyond Inferno. Passing such an area of undecontaminated radioactivity always makes a person queasy. I thanked God there weren't any such in England, as yet.

The street was almost empty, though I was accosted by a couple of beggars with faces tunneled by H-bomb scars, whether real or of makeup putty, I couldn't tell. A fat woman held out a baby with webbed fingers and toes. I told myself it would have been deformed anyway and that she was only capitalizing on our fear of bomb-induced mutations. Still, I gave her a seven-and-a-half-cent piece. Her mask made me feel I was paying tribute to an African fetish.

"May all your children be blessed with one head and two eyes, sir."

"Thanks," I said, shuddering, and hurried past her.

"... There's only trash behind the mask, so turn your head, stick to your task: Stay away, stay away—from—the—girls!"

*

This last was the end of an anti-sex song being sung by some religionists half a block from the circle-and-cross insignia of a femalist temple. They reminded me only faintly of our small tribe of British monastics. Above their heads was a jumble of billboards advertising predigested foods, wrestling instruction, radio handies and the like.

I stared at the hysterical slogans with disagreeable fascination. Since the female face and form have been banned on American signs, the very letters of the advertiser's alphabet have begun to crawl with sex—the fat-bellied, big-breasted capital B, the lascivious double O. However, I reminded myself, it is chiefly the mask that so strangely accents sex in America.

A British anthropologist has pointed out, that, while it took more than 5,000 years to shift the chief point of sexual interest from the hips to the breasts, the next transition to the face has taken less than 50 years. Comparing the American style with Moslem tradition is not valid; Moslem women are compelled to wear veils, the purpose of which is concealment, while American women have only the compulsion of fashion and use masks to create mystery.

Theory aside, the actual origins of the trend are to be found in the anti-radiation clothing of World War III, which led to masked wrestling, now a fantastically popular sport, and that in turn led to the current female fashion. Only a wild style at first, masks quickly became as necessary as brassieres and lipsticks had been earlier in the century.

I finally realized that I was not speculating about masks in general, but about what lay behind one in particular. That's the devil of the things; you're never sure whether a girl is heightening loveliness or hiding ugliness. I pictured a cool, pretty face in which fear showed only in widened eyes. Then I remembered her blonde hair, rich against the blackness of the satin mask. She'd told me to come at the twenty-second hour—ten p.m.

I climbed to my apartment near the British Consulate; the elevator shaft had been shoved out of plumb by an old blast, a nuisance in these tall New York buildings. Before it occurred to me that I would be going out again, I automatically tore a tab from the film strip under my shirt. I developed it just to be sure. It showed that the total radiation I'd taken that day was still within the safety limit. I'm not phobic about it, as so many people are these days, but there's no point in taking chances.

I flopped down on the day bed and stared at the silent speaker and the dark screen of the video set. As always, they made me think, somewhat bitterly, of the two great nations of the world. Mutilated by each other, yet still strong, they were crippled giants poisoning the planet with their dreams of an impossible equality and an impossible success.

I fretfully switched on the speaker. By luck, the newscaster was talking excitedly of the prospects of a bumper wheat crop, sown by planes across a dust bowl moistened by seeded rains. I listened carefully to the rest of the program (it was remarkably clear of Russian telejamming) but there was no further news of interest to me. And, of course, no mention of the Moon, though everyone knows that America and Russia are racing to develop their primary bases into fortresses capable of mutual assault and the launching of alphabet-bombs toward Earth. I myself knew perfectly well that the British electronic equipment I was helping trade for American wheat was destined for use in spaceships.

*

I switched off the newscast. It was growing dark and once again I pictured a tender, frightened face behind a mask. I hadn't had a date since England. It's exceedingly difficult to become acquainted with a girl in America, where as little as a smile, often, can set one of them yelping for the police—to say nothing of the increasing puritanical morality and the roving gangs that keep most women indoors after dark. And naturally, the masks which are definitely not, as the Soviets claim, a last invention of capitalist degeneracy, but a sign of great psychological insecurity. The Russians have no masks, but they have their own signs of stress.

I went to the window and impatiently watched the darkness gather. I was getting very restless. After a while a ghostly violet cloud appeared to the south. My hair rose. Then I laughed. I had momentarily fancied it a radiation from the crater of the Hell-bomb, though I should instantly have known it was only the radio-induced glow in the sky over the amusement and residential area south of Inferno.

Promptly at twenty-two hours I stood before the door of my unknown girl friend's apartment. The electronic say-who-please said just that. I answered clearly, "Wysten Turner," wondering if she'd given my name to the mechanism. She evidently had, for the door opened. I walked into a small empty living room, my heart pounding a bit.

The room was expensively furnished with the latest pneumatic hassocks and sprawlers. There were some midgie books on the table. The one I picked up was the standard hard-boiled detective story in which two female murderers go gunning for each other.

The television was on. A masked girl in green was crooning a love song. Her right hand held something that blurred off into the foreground. I saw the set had a handie, which we haven't in England as yet, and curiously thrust my hand into the handie orifice beside the screen. Contrary to my expectations, it was not like slipping into a pulsing rubber glove, but rather as if the girl on the screen actually held my hand.

A door opened behind me. I jerked out my hand with as guilty a reaction as if I'd been caught peering through a keyhole.

She stood in the bedroom doorway. I think she was trembling. She was wearing a gray fur coat, white-speckled, and a gray velvet evening mask with shirred gray lace around the eyes and mouth. Her fingernails twinkled like silver.

It hadn't occurred to me that she'd expect us to go out.

"I should have told you," she said softly. Her mask veered nervously toward the books and the screen and the room's dark corners. "But I can't possibly talk to you here."

I said doubtfully, "There's a place near the Consulate...."

"I know where we can be together and talk," she said rapidly. "If you don't mind."

As we entered the elevator I said, "I'm afraid I dismissed the cab."

*

But the cab driver hadn't gone for some reason of his own. He jumped out and smirkingly held the front door open for us. I told him we preferred to sit in back. He sulkily opened the rear door, slammed it after us, jumped in front and slammed the door behind him.

My companion leaned forward. "Heaven," she said.

The driver switched on the turbine and televisor.

"Why did you ask if I were a British subject?" I said, to start the conversation.

She leaned away from me, tilting her mask close to the window. "See the Moon," she said in a quick, dreamy voice.

"But why, really?" I pressed, conscious of an irritation that had nothing to do with her.

"It's edging up into the purple of the sky."

"And what's your name?"

"The purple makes it look yellower."

*

Just then I became aware of the source of my irritation. It lay in the square of writhing light in the front of the cab beside the driver.

I don't object to ordinary wrestling matches, though they bore me, but I simply detest watching a man wrestle a woman. The fact that the bouts are generally "on the level," with the man greatly outclassed in weight and reach and the masked females young and personable, only makes them seem worse to me.

"Please turn off the screen," I requested the driver.

He shook his head without looking around. "Uh-uh, man," he said. "They've been grooming that babe for weeks for this bout with Little Zirk."

Infuriated, I reached forward, but my companion caught my arm. "Please," she whispered frightenedly, shaking her head.

I settled back, frustrated. She was closer to me now, but silent and for a few moments I watched the heaves and contortions of the powerful masked girl and her wiry masked opponent on the screen. His frantic scrambling at her reminded me of a male spider.

I jerked around, facing my companion. "Why did those three men want to kill you?" I asked sharply.

The eyeholes of her mask faced the screen. "Because they're jealous of me," she whispered.

"Why are they jealous?"

She still didn't look at me. "Because of him."

"Who?"

She didn't answer.

I put my arm around her shoulders. "Are you afraid to tell me?" I asked. "What *is* the matter?"

She still didn't look my way. She smelled nice.

"See here," I said laughingly, changing my tactics, "you really should tell me something about yourself. I don't even know what you look like."

I half playfully lifted my hand to the band of her neck. She gave it an astonishingly swift slap. I pulled it away in sudden pain. There were four tiny indentations on the back. From one of them a tiny bead of blood welled out as I watched. I looked at her silver fingernails and saw they were actually delicate and pointed metal caps.

"I'm dreadfully sorry," I heard her say, "but you frightened me. I thought for a moment you were going to...."

At last she turned to me. Her coat had fallen open. Her evening dress was Cretan Revival, a bodice of lace beneath and supporting the breasts without covering them.

"Don't be angry," she said, putting her arms around my neck. "You were wonderful this afternoon."

The soft gray velvet of her mask, molding itself to her cheek, pressed mine. Through the mask's lace the wet warm tip of her tongue touched my chin.

"I'm not angry," I said. "Just puzzled and anxious to help."

The cab stopped. To either side were black windows bordered by spears of broken glass. The sickly purple light showed a few ragged figures slowly moving toward us.

The driver muttered, "It's the turbine, man. We're grounded." He sat there hunched and motionless. "Wish it had happened somewhere else."

My companion whispered, "Five dollars is the usual amount."

She looked out so shudderingly at the congregating figures that I suppressed my indignation and did as she suggested. The driver took the bill without a word. As he started up, he put his hand out the window and I heard a few coins clink on the pavement.

My companion came back into my arms, but her mask faced the television screen, where the tall girl had just pinned the convulsively kicking Little Zirk.

"I'm so frightened," she breathed.

*

Heaven turned out to be an equally ruinous neighborhood, but it had a club with an awning and a huge doorman uniformed like a spaceman, but in gaudy colors. In my sensuous daze I rather liked it all. We stepped out of the cab just as a drunken old woman came down the sidewalk, her mask awry. A couple ahead of us turned their heads from the half revealed face, as if from an ugly body at the beach. As we followed them in I heard the doorman say, "Get along, grandma, and watch yourself."

Inside, everything was dimness and blue glows. She had said we could talk here, but I didn't see how. Besides the inevitable chorus of sneezes and coughs (they say America is fifty per cent allergic these days), there was a band going full blast in the latest robop style, in which an electronic composing machine selects an arbitrary sequence of tones into which the musicians weave their raucous little individualities.

Most of the people were in booths. The band was behind the bar. On a small platform beside them, a girl was dancing, stripped to her mask. The little cluster of men at the shadowy far end of the bar weren't looking at her.

We inspected the menu in gold script on the wall and pushed the buttons for breast of chicken, fried shrimps and two scotches. Moments later, the serving bell tinkled. I opened the gleaming panel and took out our drinks.

*

The cluster of men at the bar filed off toward the door, but first they stared around the room. My companion had just thrown back her coat. Their look lingered on our booth. I noticed that there were three of them.

The band chased off the dancing girl with growls. I handed my companion a straw and we sipped our drinks.

"You wanted me to help you about something," I said. "Incidentally, I think you're lovely."

She nodded quick thanks, looked around, leaned forward. "Would it be hard for me to get to England?"

"No," I replied, a bit taken aback. "Provided you have an American passport."

"Are they difficult to get?"

"Rather," I said, surprised at her lack of information. "Your country doesn't like its nationals to travel, though it isn't quite as stringent as Russia."

"Could the British Consulate help me get a passport?"

"It's hardly their...."

"Could you?"

I realized we were being inspected. A man and two girls had paused opposite our table. The girls were tall and wolfish-looking, with spangled masks. The man stood jauntily between them like a fox on its hind legs.

My companion didn't glance at them, but she sat back. I noticed that one of the girls had a big yellow bruise on her forearm. After a moment they walked to a booth in the deep shadows.

"Know them?" I asked. She didn't reply. I finished my drink. "I'm not sure you'd like England," I said. "The austerity's altogether different from your American brand of misery."

She leaned forward again. "But I must get away," she whispered.

"Why?" I was getting impatient.

"Because I'm so frightened."

There were chimes. I opened the panel and handed her the fried shrimps. The sauce on my breast of chicken was a delicious steaming compound of almonds, soy and ginger. But something must have been wrong with the radionic oven that had thawed and heated it, for at the first bite I crunched a kernel of ice in the meat. These delicate mechanisms need constant repair and there aren't enough mechanics.

I put down my fork. "What are you really scared of?" I asked her.

For once her mask didn't waver away from my face. As I waited I could feel the fears gathering without her naming them, tiny dark shapes swarming through the curved night outside, converging on the radioactive pest spot of New York, dipping into the margins of the purple. I felt a sudden rush of sympathy, a desire to protect the girl opposite me. The warm feeling added itself to the infatuation engendered in the cab.

"Everything," she said finally.

I nodded and touched her hand.

"I'm afraid of the Moon," she began, her voice going dreamy and brittle as it had in the cab. "You can't look at it and not think of guided bombs."

"It's the same Moon over England," I reminded her.

"But it's not England's Moon any more. It's ours and Russia's. You're not responsible."

I pressed her hand.

"Oh, and then," she said with a tilt of her mask, "I'm afraid of the cars and the gangs and the loneliness and Inferno. I'm afraid of the lust that undresses your face. And—" her voice hushed—"I'm afraid of the wrestlers."

"Yes?" I prompted softly after a moment.

*

Her mask came forward. "Do you know something about the wrestlers?" she asked rapidly. "The ones that wrestle women, I mean. They often lose, you know. And then they have to have a girl to take their frustration out on. A girl who's soft and weak and terribly frightened. They need that, to keep them men. Other men don't want them to have a girl. Other men want them just to fight women and be heroes. But they must have a girl. It's horrible for her."

I squeezed her fingers tighter, as if courage could be transmitted—granting I had any. "I think I can get you to England," I said.

Shadows crawled onto the table and stayed there. I looked up at the three men who had been at the end of the bar. They were the men I had seen in the big coupe. They wore black sweaters and close-fitting black trousers. Their faces were as expressionless as dopers. Two of them stood above me. The other loomed over the girl.

"Drift off, man," I was told. I heard the other inform the girl: "We'll wrestle a fall, sister. What shall it be? Judo, slapsie or kill-who-can?"

I stood up. There are times when an Englishman simply must be mal-treated. But just then the foxlike man came gliding in like the star of a ballet. The reaction of the other three startled me. They were acutely embarrassed.

He smiled at them thinly. "You won't win my favor by tricks like this," he said.

"Don't get the wrong idea, Zirk," one of them pleaded.

"I will if it's right," he said. "She told me what you tried to do this afternoon. That won't endear you to me, either. Drift."

They backed off awkwardly. "Let's get out of here," one of them said loudly, as they turned. "I know a place where they fight naked with knives."

*

Little Zirk laughed musically and slipped into the seat beside my companion. She shrank from him, just a little. I pushed my feet back, leaned forward.

"Who's your friend, baby?" he asked, not looking at her.

She passed the question to me with a little gesture. I told him.

"British," he observed. "She's been asking you about getting out of the country? About passports?" He smiled pleasantly. "She likes to start running away. Don't you, baby?" His small hand began to stroke her wrist, the fingers bent a little, the tendons ridged, as if he were about to grab and twist.

"Look here," I said sharply. "I have to be grateful to you for ordering off those bullies, but—"

"Think nothing of it," he told me. "They're no harm except when they're behind steering wheels. A well-trained fourteen-year-old girl could cripple any one of them. Why, even Theda here, if she went in for that sort of thing...." He turned to her, shifting his hand from her wrist to her hair. He stroked it, letting the strands slip slowly through his fingers. "You know I lost tonight, baby, don't you?" he said softly.

I stood up. "Come along," I said to her. "Let's leave."

*

She just sat there. I couldn't even tell if she was trembling. I tried to read a message in her eyes through the mask.

"I'll take you away," I said to her. "I can do it. I really will."

He smiled at me. "She'd like to go with you," he said. "Wouldn't you, baby?"

"Will you or won't you?" I said to her. She still just sat there.

He slowly knotted his fingers in her hair.

"Listen, you little vermin," I snapped at him, "Take your hands off her."

He came up from the seat like a snake. I'm no fighter. I just know that the more scared I am, the harder and straighter I hit. This time I was lucky. But as he crumpled back, I felt a slap and four stabs of pain in my cheek. I clapped my hand to it. I could feel the four gashes made by her dagger finger caps, and the warm blood oozing out from them.

She didn't look at me. She was bending over little Zirk and cuddling her mask to his cheek and crooning: "There, there, don't feel bad, you'll be able to hurt me afterward."

There were sounds around us, but they didn't come close. I leaned forward and ripped the mask from her face.

I really don't know why I should have expected her face to be anything else. It was very pale, of course, and there weren't any cosmetics. I suppose there's no point in wearing any under a mask. The eye-brows were untidy and the lips chapped. But as for the general expression, as for the feelings crawling and wriggling across it—

Have you ever lifted a rock from damp soil? Have you ever watched the slimy white grubs?

I looked down at her, she up at me. "Yes, you're so frightened, aren't you?" I said sarcastically. "You dread this little nightly drama, don't you? You're scared to death."

And I walked right out into the purple night, still holding my hand to my bleeding cheek. No one stopped me, not even the girl wrestlers. I wished I could tear a tab from under my shirt, and test it then and there, and find I'd taken too much radiation, and so be able to ask to cross the Hudson and go down New Jersey, past the lingering radiance of the Narrows Bomb, and so on to Sandy Hook to wait for the rusty ship that would take me back over the seas to England.

www.ingramcontent.com/pod-product-compliance
Lightning Source LLC
Chambersburg PA
CBHW030416310726
48979CB00002B/439

* 9 7 9 8 8 8 0 9 0 3 2 5 2 *